B&T 5.65

IN GRANDPA'S HOUSE

PHILIP SENDAK

In Grandpa's House

———⚬∽∞∾⚬———

TRANSLATED AND ADAPTED BY

SEYMOUR BAROFSKY

PICTURES BY

MAURICE SENDAK

Harper & Row, Publishers

New York

In Grandpa's House
Text and translation copyright © 1985 by Natalie Lesselbaum
Illustrations copyright © 1985 by Maurice Sendak
Printed in the U.S.A. All rights reserved.
LC 85-42625
Trade ISBN 0-06-025462-9
Harpercrest ISBN 0-06-025463-7
Designed by Constance Fogler
First Edition

J
S

In memory of my beloved wife, Sarah

IN GRANDPA'S HOUSE

In THE TOWN where I was born, in Mishinitz, in Poland, after *heder* I listened to stories told in the *shul*, stories about dead people rising from the graves in the nearby cemetery. The stories frightened the children, and after school, when it was dark, the teacher's helper had to guide us past the graveyard with a lantern.

My father's name was Israel; my mother's, Bluma. I was the third of five children, three boys and two girls. We brothers fought all the time.

My papa was president of our town's *shul*. When I was very young, a new rabbi came. He preached against a group of intelligent men who met in the synagogue. My papa supported these men and asked the rabbi to resign. The rabbi was angry with Papa and left town, saying that our village would not have any joy from its children.

After the rabbi left, I came down with typhoid, and so did my brothers and sisters. My littlest sister died. Mama cried and pleaded with my father to find the rabbi and lift the curse. But Papa said no; instead, we moved to the *shtetl* of Zembrova, where my father's father lived and where I grew up.

Ours was a beautiful town. It had a central marketplace, and every Thursday the peasants came to buy and trade. In winter I would skate on a large pond behind our house. Khaytcha, a girl my age, skated with me. We fell in love.

Khaytcha was apprenticed to a tailor, studying to be a seamstress. Two of her brothers lived in Philadelphia, and she wanted to go to America, too. But her father refused to let her. Finally, after much quarreling, he relented.

After Khaytcha left, I wanted to follow. My father flew into a rage. I argued with Papa, but he wouldn't listen. As a result, I wanted to leave home. Because the whole town was like family, I was able to arrange to hire a droshky, even though

I had no money. When my brother saw that I was leaving, he tried to stop me by yelling and hitting. I sprang into the droshky and ran off to my mother's father, my grandfather in Mishinitz.

I wrote Papa and begged him to let me go to America. Finally, Grandpa pleaded for me, and Papa sent my sister with money for the trip.

I left for America from Mishinitz, and I have never said good-bye to my mother and father.

I arrived in New York on July 8, 1913, on the ship *President Grant*. I went to Philadelphia. Khaytcha was married. Her brothers didn't let her write to tell me. So I returned to New York, where I worked as a tucker in a shirtwaist factory.

I was doing very well. Hymie, a *landsman*, was getting married. Everyone came with presents to the wedding. It was there that I met your mama.

Mama read aloud from Sholom Aleichem, and I went up to her and talked with her and with her friends. I courted Mama every Saturday and Sunday, and in May we went to City Hall, Bronx, for a marriage license.

Mama and I first took a room in Williamsburg, Brooklyn. Then we rented three rooms in East New York, on Livonia Avenue, and bought furniture.

Natalie was born. She became sick. She coughed and turned blue, and Mama was very frightened. Natalie had the whooping cough. Every day she nearly died. I took her to Coney Island for the air. After a while she began to recover.

I became foreman at Keller's factory, and then, with Braverman and London, I left to start our own factory, which we called Lucky Stitching.

Jackie was born. He looked like an old man, thin and homely. Then he grew more beautiful.

Four years later Wall Street crashed, and because business was bad, our factory had to close down. I went to look for a job again.

Maurice was born. Dr. Brummer said the child would not have a natural birth. The doctor put his instruments in a big pot and boiled them. With the tongs he took the little head and turned it, and Maurice came out all by himself. That was the only time that I saw how a child is born. Maurice's laugh was a little bell.

We moved: West 6th Street, Kings Highway, West 4th Street, 58th Street, 18th Avenue.

I lived my whole life in Brooklyn, and everything was alright. My wife was never ill. Now I am alone. I have lost my wife, and everything is a blank to me. When I close my eyes, I see her and she wants to talk. I ask her what she wants, but she doesn't answer.

My children try to make me forget. My son asks me to write a children's story. I have tried many times, but nothing comes. When I was young, I heard so many stories and was able to tell wonderful tales. Now that I am seventy-five, I can no longer imagine myself in a child's life.

But since I have nothing else to do, I will write a story that my father told us when I was a child.

"Little children, be still! I will tell you a story,"

my papa would say. And when it was quiet, and the children opened their mouths and ears, he began his tale.

WHEN DAVID WAS a little boy, his grandfather was with him all the time, and he loved Grandpa very much.

Once David told his parents that he wanted to visit Grandpa. But they wouldn't allow him to go. David didn't obey and went alone.

He and Grandpa spent the whole day together. They took a walk, and Grandpa introduced David to his friends. When David's papa and mama found out where he was, they became very angry and scolded him.

Grandpa said to them, "But he wanted to see me, and you shouldn't be angry with him for that."

David's mother was very annoyed, and David's father looked at *his* father and said, "You lead your life, let us lead ours."

David was upset, but his grandfather said to him, "You must do whatever your father says, because your father loves you."

After that David and his father would visit Grandpa, until, once, men came and took David's grandfather away, and Grandpa never came back.

One day, shortly after David's grandfather went away, David came home from school and discovered his house empty. He called Papa and Mama, but no one answered. He was frightened and ran out into the street crying. He walked and he cried, and he didn't know what to do.

When it became dark, David sat down. He thought of his grandfather, who used to be with him all the time. Then, when Mama and Papa went away, David was not alone. He remembered how Grandpa told him stories at night.

Now David sat by himself in the dark and cried. Where had Mama and Papa gone?

All at once David saw a very big bird. The bird

swooped down and landed beside him. "Why are you crying, little boy?" asked the bird.

"I cannot find Papa and Mama," said David.

"Sit on me. I've been sent to help you."

David climbed onto the bird, and they flew away.

They flew through the dark night until morning. When it became light, David saw that they were flying above mountains and valleys.

While they were flying over one high mountain, a hand rose up out of it and took David into its palm. David was very frightened, but a voice said, "Don't be afraid. Tell me where you are flying."

"I'm looking for my parents," David answered.

The giant fixed his big eyes on David and asked, "Little boy, are you hungry?" He tore a banana from a tree, a banana so big that David couldn't hold it. The giant had to break off a little piece for him.

While David was eating, the giant told him about mighty monsters who lived on the other side of the mountain. They had horribly large heads and mon-

strous mouths and terrible teeth and very big arms. They ate so much that they kept growing. Whenever they needed more food, they came and took it, for everyone was afraid of them, and no one would stop them.

Suddenly, as they were talking, they heard the monsters coming to attack. The giant ordered his giants to march against the monsters. There was a terrible battle. Many were killed. The monsters were defeated.

Some fled, but other monsters lay on the ground bleeding and tired. When they started to get up, all at once they began to get smaller and smaller. They became very happy and kissed David and the giants and thanked them, for, they explained, they had never wanted to be monsters. They had once been small. In those days, they didn't have much food and ate only what little they had or could find. Then they discovered how to get more food and started eating and eating. They ate so much that they got bigger and bigger and had to start taking food from other people and from the giants, for they always needed more. Now that they were back to their normal size, they would live in peace.

After David had been with the giants for some time, he flew away on the bird to continue the search for his parents.

David and the bird were flying over water when a great storm broke out. The storm became fiercer and fiercer. All at once, David fell into the mouth of a big fish. He thought, "I am lost and will never see Papa and Mama." But then he realized that the fish wasn't hurting him.

David started to walk around in the belly of the fish. He looked through the fish's eyes and saw many beautiful fish of different colors and shapes. He also saw how the fish were swallowing each other, big ones swallowing little ones. David began talking to a little fish who had been swallowed along with him.

"Is it always like this in the sea?" he asked.

"No," he answered. "We also live in families that are good and protect each other."

The little fish then told David many stories about his life. He had a family and many children and they always had to fight off big fish. Then he said, "I don't know if I'll survive this one." But the little fish wasn't afraid, because he had many grown children who would continue to fight.

As David listened to the little fish, he saw that they were swimming through such wonder-ful places, between mountains and valleys. David couldn't stop wondering at the beauty. Suddenly, he saw a fish much bigger than the one who had swallowed him. As soon as his fish saw this bigger fish, he turned to flee. David pleaded with the fish to spit him out. The fish said, "Alright, I will spit you out; that will make it easier for *me* to get away." Then he spit him very far onto the shore.

He also spit out the little fish he had swallowed with David onto the land. David grabbed the little fish and ran to the water's edge to throw it back into the sea. But it was too late. The fish had already died. So David considered what to do. To throw the fish back, he thought, what good would that do? He knew that the little fish would have wanted David to eat it since he was so hungry. So he cooked the fish and ate it.

The bird had been flying over the water all this time, waiting for David. After David rested awhile, he called the bird, and they flew away.

As they were flying, David heard shots. The bird landed, and David leaped off the bird. In the distance men were racing away on horseback. David followed to see what was happening. He came to a camp where he saw many people lying on the ground. Others—men, women, and children—were arriving. They were being driven by men on horses carrying big whips. The people all lay on the ground surrounded by the men with whips. David was frightened. He waited quietly and watched. Then the guards made everyone rise and drove them all into a cave. Each was given a shovel and made to work.

David knew that they were slaves. One of the guards rode back and forth and looked around. He seemed to be the leader. David became afraid that he would be caught and made a slave too. So, slowly and quietly, he crept away.

When he got far enough into the hills, he entered a cave to rest, for he was very tired and still frightened. Just as he lay down, he heard a noise and then saw a man coming toward him. David jumped up in terror, but the man quickly said, "Don't be afraid. I won't harm you."

He approached, and David asked, "Who are you?"

"I live here," the man answered.

"And who are those people I saw in the valley working in the mine?"

"They were kidnaped," the man said, "and forced to work for the men on horseback. I, too, was once a slave," he added, "but I ran away from the master and hid in this cave. In the cave I found a lion. The lion had a thorn in his paw and was in great pain. I was filled with fear, and I didn't dare stir. I was afraid to approach the lion and afraid that if I left the cave, I would be made a slave again. After a while I became a little bolder and moved nearer the lion. Then I went up to him and lifted his paw, and pulled out the big thorn. I became so brave that I could help even a lion, I thought. And I wasn't afraid of the slavemaster anymore.

"I have been living here ever since," the man continued. "I like to be a free man; I don't like to be a slave."

After David had rested for a bit, he went looking for the bird. He was hungry. Soon he came to a beautiful forest. He walked into it in search of fruit trees, so that he could eat something.

It was dark and eerie in the thick woods. Suddenly David felt something, and then someone attacked him. He felt lots of hands pulling at him.

All of a sudden everything went black. Whoever had attacked him had thrown a sack over his head and tied up the end so that David was trapped inside. Then they started dragging him.

They pulled David for some distance, bumping him along the ground. After they arrived someplace and they stopped moving, David could hear the voices of many people.

Someone opened the sack and David crawled out carefully. He found himself in a large cave, sur-rounded by many people. What was strange was that the people were all very, very small. David looked at the crowd of tiny people, and he asked, "What do you want from me?"

They started, all together, to scream at him: "Why have you come here? You've come to steal from us."

David was frightened by the outburst and didn't know what to say. "You are bigger than us," the tiny people yelled at him, "and you want to take our jewels."

David pleaded with them and said that he didn't even know they had any valuables, that he had come looking for food only, because he was hungry.

"But we have hardly any food here," they screeched. "Only diamonds and gold."

As they were speaking, David looked around and realized that the walls of the cave were glittering and shiny, that they were made of diamonds and gold.

"I don't want your diamonds," he said. "I wanted only to stop for something to eat, for I am hungry."

"We have so little for ourselves," the tiny people shouted back.

"Why don't you buy some if you have all these diamonds and gold?" David asked. "Let me have one small bit, and I will bring you food."

"You want to trick us, to take our gold and run away."

"No," David said. "I want to help you."

David then saw a stick on the ground. "Let me

show you something," he said. He picked up the stick and made an arrow of it. Then he found another twig and took some string from his pocket and fashioned a bow. In the sky, birds were flying by, and he shot until he hit one. He knew how to cook chicken and bake from having watched his mother. So he built a fire and cooked the bird and gave it to the little people to eat. They were amazed, and they huddled together in a conference. When they looked up at David again, they said that they had agreed to let him have some gold with which to buy them other food.

David took the gold and ran through the forest until he came to a town at its outskirts. There he bought bread and milk and fruit. He ate some and brought the rest to the little people. They began eating at once, and as they ate all the different foods, they grew taller and taller, until they were no longer little people.

They were very happy, because they weren't afraid anymore that bigger people would take their jewels and gold. They were so pleased that they took a handful of diamonds and gold and gave it to David as a gift before he returned to the bird to fly on in search of his parents.

David grew very tired and asked the bird to land near a town that he had seen from above.

It was a town of olden times. The women were sitting at a stream and washing their laundry. The houses were simple huts. David went up to one, knocked, and entered. Inside, a sick man lay in bed. The man didn't have anyone to care for his sheep, he said. Here each household has a flock of sheep, and every morning shepherds take them to the fields to graze.

A woman entered the room and said to David, "Come, I will give you some food." After he had eaten, she led him outside and shouted, "King!"

A big dog ran up, and the woman told it to gather the sheep and go with David to the fields. David would learn to be a shepherd.

When they found a grazing place, David sat down on a rock. Other shepherds came by. They practiced shooting bows and arrows.

When David returned from the fields, the woman told him to go to the town school. He went to a house where children were sitting around a long table. An old man was telling them stories, and David listened. The man also taught them how to read and write, and they studied Torah.

In the morning, David and the dog King set out to graze the sheep. King and David became good friends. David would pet King, and King would look at him as if he wanted to speak. As they were sitting, they heard a sudden great noise. Wild animals came from behind the rocks at the edge of the field. They ran at the sheep.

David leaped for his bow and arrows, and King ran to help the sheep that were being attacked. David started shooting, and finally the animals were driven away.

After they fled, David called King, but there was

no answer. Then he saw King, lying on the ground. King was dead; he had been killed in the fight with the animals.

David cried and cried when he saw that he had lost his good friend King. He wept again when he told the man and woman back in town what had happened. They bought another dog, but David never stopped missing King. Then it was time again for David to continue the search for his parents. He called the bird, and they flew away.

They flew until it grew dark.

Then the bird said, "Since it is dark, I will take you someplace for the night."

They came to a thick woods. In the woods there was a wonderful palace, and it was all lit up and shone in the dark. It was a very, very big house. The bird came down near a door, and David jumped off its back.

David opened the door and went in. He was astounded. He had never seen anything like it. It

was so bright and beautiful, and it was full of angels. He walked and walked through the house until he came to a large room. In the center of the room was a very long table, and around the table sat old people with beards. David went up to an old man who sat at the head of the table. As soon as he saw the little boy, the old man said, "David, come here! Do you know who I am?"

David looked and looked but was not sure. Then all of a sudden he recognized him and ran into his arms, crying, "Oh, Grandpa, I'm so happy to see you. But I've been looking for Papa and Mama. Where have they gone? So many things have happened to me."

"I know, and that is why I sent the bird to help you," said Grandpa. "The bird took you first to the giants and the monsters to teach you that people, even little people, who keep wanting more and more will turn into monsters.

"Then he took you to the world of the fish, so that you would learn that there are worlds where the big eat the little, and that man must not live like an animal.

"Next he took you to meet the runaway slave to teach you not to fear.

"Then you were captured by the tiny people, where you saw that if you eat properly, you will grow big and strong—and that is better than diamonds and gold.

"And, finally, the bird carried you to the ancient village, where you learned that man has to work as well as study, and where you lost King, a good friend, who can never be replaced. That is why I once gave you a puppy as a gift, and you took care of it and loved it and gave him a name. God made animals to help man, and grandparents should buy grandchildren little dogs as presents."

"Oh, Grandpa," said David.

"Now let me show you where you are." With that, Grandpa took David by the hand and led him through the long, long corridors of the big house.

Finally, they came to an enormous black door. They entered and stood in a large room before a big table. Three bearded old men sat behind the table. They called out, "Samuel!" And Samuel, the rabbi of our town, entered.

The three men accused Samuel of having fooled the people of the town into believing that he was a learned man when he was not. And he cheated them.

"Why should *I* be guilty," Samuel answered his accusers, "because *they* believed me?"

The three bearded men ordered: "Open the doors of Hell! For telling lies, burn his tongue. For cheating, burn him all over. Burn him and broil him seven times, then let him be."

They called Satan, who grabbed Samuel and threw him into the fire of Hell. Samuel screamed, and Satan took him out and threw him back again.

Grandpa then grasped David's hand again and they left this room. They walked for a very long time through the bright and sparkling corridors of the big house. They came to a huge white door and walked through.

Inside was a very large round table. Old men with white beards and dressed all in white sat around it. They were studying Torah, and their faces were aglow.

Grandpa walked up to the table. There was a seat there for him. He turned to David and said, "This is a place for old people. When we come here, our children take our places. But you, my child, don't belong here. Don't be afraid. Your papa is not here any longer either.

"Now I will tell you what happened to your papa and mama. Because your papa was very poor, he was ashamed. He and Mama made friends with bad people. They ran away to another town. They planned to steal to get money. They broke into a house. But the people who owned the house had been warned, and they waited for them, and Mama and Papa were killed.

"In that way they came here. But I begged the judges to forgive them because Papa was poor. And the judges did not send them to the terrible angel who waits to punish bad people. Instead, the judges decided to let them return to you, because I told the judges that you need your papa and mama.

"They are home now. They are worried because they cannot find you, and they do not know that I sent the bird to take you on this journey.

"Go home and help them with the reward that I know the little people gave you. When Papa and Mama have the money, they will help the poor and build a synagogue. You will go to school and be a good student. One day you will fall in love and have a beautiful wedding. And Papa will be so happy when you have your first child. Papa and Mama will help their grandchild. They learned that from Grandpa. And the child will love them.

"You will never forget me, even though you become rich and famous."

David looked at the old men around the table as

Grandpa spoke. They were all smiling brightly as they continued to study Torah.

"Your grandpa is very happy, too," said David's grandfather.

David felt as if he were melting with joy.

As they were talking the sun came up, and everything started slowly to disappear, until all was gone—the old people and the big house with the long table.

Only the bird remained, and it called out to David, "Sit on me, and I will take you home."

David climbed up on the bird, and the bird flew him home, where his papa and mama were anxiously waiting.

About the text

When Philip Sendak (1894-1970) was an old and sick man, his son Maurice suggested that they collaborate on a book. Philip Sendak's attempt at writing stories resulted in eighty-nine handwritten pages. Those pages contain three different children's stories, none completed, and a reminiscence of his own life, also unfinished. The manuscript, fairly closely written in the Americanism-rich Yiddish of New York's immigrant community, is the source of most of the material in this book. In addition, Maurice Sendak made available some biographical notes his father had dictated, some of his father's letters, and a notebook of exercises his father had written toward the end of his life in an effort to improve his English. Some sentences based on these are also now part of *In Grandpa's House*.

In his way, Philip Sendak typifies his generation in these un-self-conscious writings. The immigrant faced a double loss: of his parents in a vanished world; of his children in a new one, a world largely made, he knew, by his own efforts, yet in which he could never fully share. When Philip Sendak wrote these pages, he wanted to use them to teach, to exert his rightful influence on the future. He had had neither opportunity nor time to develop the niceties of style and form. His desire to instruct, though, came naturally—from the Jew's imbibing of

Midrash and holy tale and from the immigrant's extreme social-mindedness and practicality, even in art. And aren't wisdom and honor a grandfather's natural state, too, despite any actual disappointments of old age and grandfatherhood that occasionally break through? Philip Sendak wanted to teach that a child should eat properly, study, have courage, be fair and just, and leave something for the next generation. In writing for his son, Philip Sendak had returned, finally, to the hope expressed when every infant Jewish boy is introduced into the *bris*: "that he enter into the Torah, into the *hupah* [that is, marriage], and into good deeds."

S.B.